Dinosaurs in My Basement

Deborah Lomax-Reid
"Meatball"

Illustrated by
Ed Hedgepeth
"Hedge"

To order additional copies of this book, contact:
Xlibris Corporation
1-888-795-4274
www.Xlibris.com
Orders@Xlibris.com

In loving memory of
my mom and dad,
Mary Louise
and
Rhea Swann

I woke up to a mystery noise.
I didn't know what to think.
The room was dark. I couldn't see.
My eyes began to blink.

4

I threw my legs onto the floor-
And jumped onto my feet.
A scratching noise began to screech.
My heart thumped a thousand beats

What could this be; this noise I heard?
It certainly wasn't right!
I tried to think about this sound.
I tried with all my might.

I'd better take some action here.
I knew I had to know.
So, I tipped to the threshold of the basement door,
Though I didn't want to go.

I turned the knob. I took a peek.

I tried to stay unseen.

But, what I saw just made me scream—

An eye stared back at me!

I slammed the door and locked it shut.
I ran back to my room.
My heart just thumped, I couldn't breathe
And then the house went boom!!!

A bumping and a screeching....
and a moving all about
A growling and a roaring....
And the house began to spout!!!!

Oh my goodness! What to do???

Just what was I to do?

I had to think! Think! Think! Think! Think!

And then my brain came to!!!

There's dog food in my cupboard
and cat food in the shed.
There's lots of horse food in the stalls
and treats under my bed.

I ran to all these places
just as fast as I could go.
I ran so fast I forgot to scream
even when I stumped my toe.

I filled two trash bags full of food
and stuffed my pockets full.
I threw them down the basement steps
and hoped the racket cooled.

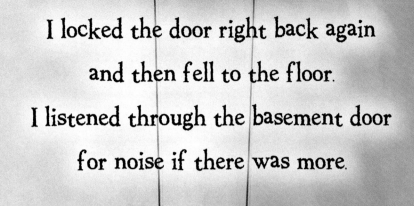

I locked the door right back again
and then fell to the floor.
I listened through the basement door
for noise if there was more.

But all I heard was quiet
and some smacking of the lips.
Some oohs, some aahs, some yum yum yums,
and scratching finger tips.

And then, after a little while,
I didn't hear a sound.
Except what sounded like some purrs
much like a sleeping hound.

So then I thought! OK I'll look!!!
I can really take a chance.
I really want to see what's there.
I'll only take a glance.

So, I opened up the basement door
and tipped right down the stairs.
My eyes got big. Would you believe?
They were sleeping dinosaurs!!!!

I forgot just for a moment
the fear inside my mind.
They looked so very cozy
and completely satisfied.

It was really quite amazing;
the scene upon the floor.
The sound of the sleeping animals
went from purring to a snore.

So, I counted all the dinosaurs
and I counted more than five.
But while I stood there counting
they seemed to come alive!

And while I stood there counting,

forgetting where I was.

They all woke up to look at me

just like a puppy does.

Their great big eyes just looked at me.

I didn't know what to think.

I got a little nervous

and my heart began to sink.

And you will not believe this,
because I really don't.
And I really don't want to tell you,
because I know you won't.
But those great big silly dinosaurs
began to lick my shoes;
as if they all were thanking me
for the treats and all the food.

The purring started up again.

Their eyes began to blink.

But, I looked a little closer.

They were really trying to wink.

The fear inside my mind was gone.

They were so quite content.

23

And so, I think I'm going to keep the dinosaurs in my basement!!!!!!!!

Edwards Brothers, Inc.
Thorofare, NJ USA
February 28, 2012